Plumeria
· PRINCESS ™ ·
and Tūtū's Magic 'Ukulele

Adapted from a concept created by D. C. Perkins
Written by Cathy East Dubowski
Illustrated by Don Robinson

ISLAND HERITAGE™
PUBLISHING

Published and distributed by

ISLAND HERITAGE™
P U B L I S H I N G
A DIVISION OF THE MADDEN CORPORATION

94-411 Kō'aki Street, Waipahu, Hawai'i 96797-2806
Orders: (800) 468-2800 • Information: (808) 564-8800
Fax: (808) 564-8877 • islandheritage.com

ISBN 1-59700-365-4
First Edition, Third Printing - 2007

Piko

Plumeria

Tūtū

Dad

Mom

Nalu

Kainoa

Trina

Manu

Kayla

Ginger

I was playing my '*ukulele*, wishing that someone in my family would say, "Hey, Plumeria, that sounds good." But as usual, nobody did.

"I'm going outside," I said. No one seemed to notice except my dog, Piko.

I practiced a song I used to sing with *Tūtū*—my grandmother. I listened for voices singing in the breeze, the voices I heard when we used to sing together, but all I could hear was my noisy brothers and sister inside and the arguing of the Slipper sisters, who lived next door. I call them the "Slipper" sisters because of the flip-flop slippers they almost always wear.

"Come on, Piko," I said, "let's go to the beach." Mom and Dad let us go alone because they knew I wouldn't go in the water past my ankles.

I tried playing and singing at the beach, but I was interrupted by my friends
Manu and Trina chasing after their soccer ball.

"Hey, Plumeria!" Trina said. "Want to play with us?"

I rolled the ball back to her.

"You're a really good singer," Manu said. "I mean you, Plumeria. Not Piko."

"Yeah, sure," I said. I blushed because I don't usually sing in front of people.

"He's right," said Trina. "You ought to enter the Song Fest contest on
Saturday. Here, I've got a flyer."

"I bet you're good enough to get first place," Manu said.

Piko woofed, and we all laughed.

"Can I keep this?" I asked.

"Sure," Trina said.

"Thanks," I said. "Come on, Piko. Let's go show this to Mom and Dad."

"Can I be in this contest?" I asked my parents.

"Fine with me," Dad said.

"It sounds like fun," said Mom.

I escaped to the living room, hoping for a little quiet so I could plan for the contest.

I touched the things that rested on *Tūtū's* special shelf. I almost felt her there, helping me decide what song to sing. I missed *Tūtū* the most of anyone in my family. After all, she gave me my name—she said I was as precious as the plumeria flower she always wore in her hair.

A minute later, my parents came in. My dad strummed *Tūtū's 'ukulele.* "This *'ukulele* sounded so heavenly when *Tūtū* played it," he said. "It must be magic, Plumeria."

That's it! I told myself. "Can I use *Tūtū's 'ukulele* in the contest?"

"I don't know, Plumeria. It's so very special. . . ."

"You can use mine," said my brother Kainoa.

"No offense," said my other brother, Nalu. "But how can she win a contest with a junky old *'ukulele* like that?"

"Please, Mom. Please, Dad—*please* let me borrow *Tūtū's 'ukulele,*" I said. "I know she'd want me to play it."

My parents looked at each other. At last my mother nodded. "*Tūtū* always said, '*No one is hurt by doing the right thing,*'" she said quietly.

I was so happy, I jumped up and down.

"But," Dad said, "you must promise to take very good care of it, Plumeria."

"I promise!" I said. "Do you want to help me practice?"

Then my baby sister Leia pushed over a stack of books and everyone forgot about the contest.

The day before the contest Piko and I went outside to pick pink and white plumeria for the lei I'd wear in the contest, along with the grass skirt *Tūtū* gave me. When my bag was full of flowers, I started to practice the song I'd chosen—*Tūtū's* song.

Suddenly I heard singing coming from the Slipper sisters' yard next door. I looked through the hibiscus hedge.

The Slipper sisters were on their *lānai* singing to music from a karaoke machine. They sounded terrific. Were they practicing for the contest, too?

All of a sudden the older one, Ginger, turned and looked right at me. "Hey—what are you doing there?" she snapped.

I went right into their yard to show them I wasn't afraid of them.

"I'm going to sing in the Song Fest," I said.

"Don't waste your time," said Ginger. "First place is *ours!*"

Ginger then looked down at Kayla. "Yeah!" Kayla replied in agreement.

"Well, I'll be playing my grandmother's magic 'ukulele!" I said.

Ginger laughed. "Magic? What a baby!" said Ginger. "Wait until the judges hear *us.*"

Ginger turned the karaoke machine back on, and the Slipper sisters sang and danced to the music, as cool as TV stars. I'd need a magic 'ukulele for sure to compete with them!

I ran straight to Trina's house. "Trina! Help! I can't compete in a lei and grass skirt. I need a makeover!"

"Don't worry," said Trina. "You can count on me."

Trina helped me try on millions of outfits from her big sister's closet, and she picked out some crazy tall shoes. Then she did my makeup. "You look totally awesome!" she said when she was done.

Piko woofed in agreement.

Wow! I couldn't even tell it was me. "The judges will be really impressed!" I said.

"Now let's work on your routine," said Trina.

"Okay." I looked around. "Wait . . . where's my 'ukulele?"

Trina helped me search for it, but we couldn't find it anywhere. "Are you sure you had it when you came over?" Trina said.

"Uh oh," I said. "I must have left it at the Slipper sisters' house! I've got to go!"

I changed back to my regular clothes and washed off the makeup, then ran all the way to the Slipper sisters' yard. No *'ukulele* in sight.

I pounded on their door. Ginger and Kayla came out.

"Have you seen my *'ukulele?*" I asked.

Ginger sneered. "You mean your 'magic' *'ukulele?*"

"Please tell me where it is!" I said. "Please!"

Kayla opened her mouth to
say something but before she could,
Ginger yanked her back inside.

"We haven't seen your stupid
'ukulele," Ginger said. "Now go away.
We have to practice!"
She slammed the
door in my face.

Piko and I walked home slowly. How could
I sing in the Song Fest without *Tūtū*'s magic
ʻukulele? And, worse yet, how could I tell
Mom and Dad it was lost?

I sneaked into my room, glad not to be noticed.

A few minutes later, Dad came in. "Hi, Plumeria. Would you like me to listen while you practice?"

I couldn't say a word. I wanted to tell my dad what happened, but the words got stuck in my throat.

I shook my head. "I should rest my voice," I whispered.

I heard the front door open, and Mom called out, "We're home!" over Leia's wailing. "And I need help with the groceries!"

Dad hurried off. For once I was happy I had a fussy baby sister.

That night I dreamed that *Tūtū* helped me find the *ʻukulele*.
It was hidden in a plumeria tree.

The next day I looked for it
again, and again I couldn't find it.

Soon it was time to get ready for
the contest.

When I told my parents I was going to
Trina's to get ready, I could hardly look at them.

"I thought *I* was going to help you," Mom said.

"But Trina and I have already picked out my
clothes, and she's even going to do my makeup."

My Dad raised his eyebrows. "Makeup?"

I nodded. "We've already tried it out, and I looked really good. You'll see."

"Okay," my parents said together, but they didn't look very happy about it.

"We'll see you there," Mom said as I left for Trina's house.

"Don't worry," Trina said when I told her the 'ukulele was still missing.
"It will turn up."

I shook my head. "Maybe I should just forget about the contest."

"No way!" said Trina. "You don't need that 'ukulele. Just sing like
you did that day at the beach."

When we arrived for the contest, Trina sat in the audience
while I went backstage to the contestants' waiting area. The
Slipper sisters were there already—and they looked great.

"Did you ever find that magic 'ukulele of yours?" Ginger asked.

Her voice sounded sugary sweet—too sweet. She was pretending to be nice, but underneath the sweetness, she was being mean. All of a sudden I realized why she was doing that. "You took it, didn't you?"

Ginger smiled. It was a smile that matched her voice—nice on the surface, but mean underneath. I knew I'd been right, and I was so mad that I couldn't stop myself from getting back at her.

"A photographer from the paper was looking for you," I said, sounding just as sweet as she had.

Ginger fluffed up her hair. "Really? Where?"

"This way," I said.

The Slipper sisters followed me down a stairway.

"In there."

The sisters rushed in, and I pushed the heavy door closed and locked them in.

"Hey, this is a closet," Ginger said. The door was so heavy that her voice was muffled. Ginger and Kayla could scream all they wanted, but no one would hear them.

My hands shook as I walked away. I knew what I'd done was mean, but I told myself they deserved it.

Almost all the seats were filled. The audience looked like a scary million-eyed creature, and I shook with nervousness. But there was Dad waving at me from the front row. I felt better—until I remembered that I didn't have *Tūtū's 'ukulele*.

A man with a clipboard came by. "Has anybody seen Ginger and Kayla?"

I stared at the floor.

"Hey, you!" He looked right at me. "You seen them?"

I just shook my head.

I swallowed hard and looked out into the audience again. Mom and Dad were smiling. Even Kainoa and Nalu looked excited. They seemed so proud of me, even before I sang my first note. I knew they wouldn't be proud, though, if they knew what I'd done.

Then I heard *Tūtū's* voice. It was almost as if she were really there with me. She was saying, *"No one is hurt by doing the right thing."*

I sighed. I knew what I had to do.

I ran over to the man with the clipboard. "I've got to do something," I said. "I'll be right back."

He shrugged. "You'd better hurry. If those sisters don't show up pretty quick, it will be your turn."

I ran to the closet and reached for the doorknob. Once I let the Slipper sisters out, they'd tell on me, and I'd probably get in BIG trouble. But *Tūtū's* words were ringing in my head. *"No one is hurt by doing the right thing."*

My heart pounded. My hands shook. I unlocked the door.

The sisters rushed out. "You're gonna get it!" Ginger shouted.

"You didn't miss anything," I said. "You're on now."

Ginger rushed off without saying anything, but Kayla stayed behind. "Why did you let us out?" she whispered. "Now my sister and I are going to beat you in the contest."

I shrugged. "I didn't want to win that way."

"Kayla!" Ginger shouted. "Come *on!*"

"In a second," Kayla said. She smiled at me—a friendly smile. "You know, Plumeria, we deserved what you did."

I stared. "What?"

"We did take your *'ukulele*. It was Ginger's idea," Kayla said. "It's in the shed in our yard, behind the bikes." Then she left.

I wanted to run to their house, but the man with the clipboard called my name. "Plumeria! Up here! You're on next."

I hurried to the wings and watched the Slipper sisters perform. When they finished the audience clapped so hard it sounded like thunder. They *were* great. I wished I could be like them.

The sisters brushed past me on their way offstage.

"Good luck," Kayla whispered. I knew she meant it.

29

I walked onstage. I felt as small as an ant. The song I'd
rehearsed, one that *Tūtū* and I used to sing on the beach under the
blue sky, didn't seem right for this glitzy stage and bright white lights.
I decided to sing another song, one I'd heard on the radio. Something more
like the Slipper sisters' song.

I tried my best, but everything went wrong. I forgot some of the words. I
tripped in Trina's sister's high-heeled shoes. My face itched from the makeup.

As soon as I finished, I ran offstage.

When the contest was over, my family came backstage where the contestants were waiting for the judges' decision.

"That was, um, an interesting song," said Dad.

"Nice job," Mom said as she eyed my outfit and makeup.

"What happened to *Tūtū's 'ukulele?*" Dad asked.

Uh oh. I'd have to explain—tell them what happened to the *'ukulele*. "Um, it's . . . " I started to say. But Nalu interrupted me.

"Hey, Plumeria," Nalu said, "is that your Halloween costume?"

I knew he was only teasing, but I was so upset about *Tūtū's 'ukulele* that I burst into tears.

"Sorry!" he said. "I was just kidding!"

Everyone hugged me and tried to make me feel better. My whole family was paying attention to me, but all I wanted was to disappear.

"Let's get out of here," I said.

We went down to a nearby beach.
I dipped my hands in the surf and tried to
scrub the makeup off my face. My tears hid in
the salty water.

I'm never going to sing again, I told myself.

Soon the sun went down.
People came down to the beach
with picnic supplies. There
was music and laughter and the
delicious smells of food on the grill.
We were invited to join in, but I
didn't feel like being at a party. I missed
my grandmother. I wondered what she
would think of me today. I remembered her
words—*No one is hurt by doing the right thing.*
I sighed.

I kicked off my shoes and wiggled my toes in the sand.

Softly, slowly, I began to sing. Not something from the radio, but one of *Tūtū*'s songs.

I didn't feel so sad and alone.

When I stopped, I heard someone behind me.

"Plumeria!" It was my mom, smiling a smile as bright as the sun. "You sing so beautifully—like a princess."

"I miss *Tūtū*," I told her. "I miss her singing."

"Me, too," Mom said. She held me tight. A tear fell from her face onto mine. "But tonight I heard her singing. She is still here."

I looked up, confused.

Mom smiled. "Yes, my precious flower—my princess. She is still here, singing through you."

Kainoa was smiling too. "Plumeria Princess," he said.

"Plumeria Princess," Nalu repeated. Then he nodded and said, "Sounds good."

Dad took my hand, and we all walked toward the party. "Would you do us the honor of singing one of the old songs?" he asked.

I looked around. Trina and Manu waved. No million-eyed creature here, just family and friends and neighbors.

I felt a tap on my shoulder.

"Here, this is yours," Kayla said. "I'm really, really sorry about what happened."

"Thanks!" I said. "I'm so glad to have it back!"

"Look what I brought," Mom said, pulling from her bag the grass skirt, hat, and lei I was supposed to wear for the contest. I put them on.

"Perfect!" said Dad.

When I played and sang, even Leia listened to me!

People sat quietly for a moment when I finished. Then they clapped and cheered. A man in a red shirt shouted. "*Hana hou*—one more time!"

As I ran my hand along the smooth wood of the *'ukulele*, I suddenly realized the magic had never been in it. The magic was in *Tūtū* when she played and sang. And now it was in me.

We all sang the next song together. My brothers really got into it, pounding out rhythms with some sticks.

After a while some people started to wander
home. Others walked down the beach. Kids started a game of
moonlight Frisbee.

Trina and Manu pulled on my hands. "Come, let's play!" they shouted.

"In a minute," I said. "I need to talk to Kayla first."

I turned to Kayla. "I'm so sorry—I forgot all about the contest. How did
you do?"

"We came in third."

"That's pretty good," I said.

Kayla shrugged. "Thanks."

We both dug our toes in the sand. I thought about next year's contest. I knew one thing for sure—if I entered again, I'd sing the right song. At least, the right one for me, Plumeria.

Then I had an idea.

"Would you like me to teach you the song I just sang?" I said.

Kayla smiled. "Would you? That would be great!"

I sang a line and she sang it back, the way *Tūtū* used to teach me. It was like tossing a Frisbee back and forth. Our voices blended like we'd been singing together forever.

As we practiced, I heard something—voices singing in the wind. Just like I used to hear when I sang with *Tūtū*. Magic. My idea had worked.

"We should sing together at the Song Fest next year," I said.

Kayla's eyes narrowed. "You want to sing with me?"

I nodded. "Yes. I do."

"Wow," said Kayla. "Okay. I'd love that."

I looked up at the moon. I imagined I saw *Tūtū's* face in its white light. Her head was tossed back and she was laughing with joy to hear the magical music we were making.

The End